Robert and the Great Pepperoni

Robert and the Great Pepperoni

by Barbara Seuling
Illustrated by Paul Brewer

For Audrey,
Robert's godmother,
who watched him grow
—B. S.

To Barbara, thanks for Robert
—P. B.

Text copyright © 2001 by Barbara Seuling
Illustrations copyright © 2001 by Paul Brewer
All rights reserved
Printed in the United States of America
Designed by Anthony Jacobson
First edition, 2001

Library of Congress Cataloging-in-Publication Data

Seuling, Barbara.
    Robert and the great Pepperoni / by Barbara Seuling ; illustrated by Paul Brewer.
        p. cm.
    Summary: Second grader Robert, who desperately wants a dog of his own, starts a
pet-sitting business, but when he finds a stray dog, the best he can do is to keep him
temporarily and train him so he can be adopted by someone else.
    ISBN 0-8126-2825-X (cloth)
    [1. Pets—Fiction. 2. Pet sitting—Fiction. 3. Dogs—Fiction. 4. Schools—Fiction.]
I. Brewer, Paul, ill. II. Title.

PZ7.S5135 Ro 2001
[Fic]—dc21

                                                            2001028854

Contents

Robert and the Great Pepperoni

Half-Price Special

Squoosh. Robert sank into his beanbag chair. His book bag slid to the floor. A book fell out.

"*'Harry the Invisible Dog,'*" read his friend Paul, picking it up. "Another dog book?"

Robert had read almost every dog book in the class library. It was taking him a long time, because he was a slow reader.

"It's the best I can do, since I can't have a dog."

"Why do you want a dog?"

"A dog wags his tail when you come home from school. He's so glad to see you, he slobbers you with kisses."

"You also have to walk him."

"I know," said Robert. "I wouldn't mind doing that."

"Why don't you walk dogs for people? Any dog will slobber on you if you let him."

Robert laughed. "That's a good idea." Paul always had good ideas. Robert tore a sheet of paper out of his notebook and wrote:

I WALK DOGS

ONE DOLLAR

"You may have to feed them, too," said Paul when Robert showed it to him.

Robert wrote:

I WALK AND FEED DOGS

ONE DOLLAR

Paul looked at it again. "What if someone has a dog and fish, too?"

Robert chewed his eraser. He wrote:

I TAKE CARE OF PETS

~~AND FEED~~

~~I WALK AND DOGS~~

ONE DOLLAR — EACH

"Should fish cost as much as dogs?"
asked Paul. "You have to walk a dog. You

4

only have to sprinkle dried flies into a fish-tank."

Paul thought of everything. Robert tore out a new sheet of paper and wrote the ad over again.

I TAKE CARE
OF PetS
ONE DOLLAR EACH
SMALL ANIMALS
HALF PRICE
CALL
ROBERT DORFMAN
TODAY

"Yeah," said Paul. He got ready to go home. "Don't forget to add your phone number."

"Right," said Robert, writing it in. He looked at his ad and smiled.

After Paul left, Robert made two more copies of the notice. He asked his mom to put one up at the Super Shopper. He asked his brother, Charlie, to put one up in the pet shop when he went to the mall with his friends. The last one went in Robert's notebook for the bulletin board at school.

Robert couldn't wait. Maybe he'd have a dog to take care of soon.

Customer Number One

"*Attack of the Lizard People!*" said Charlie.

"*Nutty Professor II*!" said Robert.

Friday was family night, when the Dorfmans ordered pizza and watched movies. Charlie liked chase scenes, explosions, and scary monsters. Robert liked movies that made him laugh. They flipped a coin. Charlie won. He popped his movie into the VCR.

A band of lizard people was fighting an army of giant grasshoppers when the phone rang.

"It's for you, Robert," called his mom. Robert didn't mind missing some of the movie. It was getting pretty gruesome. Wings and tails were flying everywhere.

"This is Esther Glass," said a woman. "Is this the person who takes care of pets?"

"Yes."

"I live on Oak Street," the woman said. Her voice was shaky. "I'm going into the hospital. Can you take care of my birds while I'm away?"

"Sure," said Robert. When he'd talked to his parents about his new business, they'd said that he could only take jobs that were close to home. Oak Street was only a few blocks away. He wrote down Mrs. Glass's address.

The next morning, Robert stopped at Mrs. Glass's to pick up her house key. She was old. Robert watched carefully as she showed him how to feed the doves and clean their cage.

"This is Billie, and this one's Flo," said Mrs. Glass. They looked exactly alike. "I'll miss them. You will take good care of them, won't you?" Robert saw tears filling her eyes.

"Yes, ma'am," he said.

Every day Robert got off the school bus a stop early to go to Mrs. Glass's house. He fed the doves. On Fridays he took extra time to clean their cage and line it with newspaper.

In school, Robert's class was preparing for Earth Day. They had to write about or draw something that was not good for the earth. Then they had to make a suggestion for fixing it.

Robert drew a picture of a truck parked by a river. A man was dumping a barrel of black stuff into the water. A police car had pulled up with its lights flashing. Nearby, in a park, a boy was drinking from a water

fountain. Over his head was a cartoon bal-
loon that read: YUCK! THIS TASTES FUNNY!

"That's so cute," said Susanne Lee
Rodgers, stretching over his shoulder to
look.

Robert didn't see how polluting a river
could be called cute.

"Thanks," he said.

"You take care of pets?"

"Uh-huh. Why?"

"I have a job for you."

Robert looked up, scratching his neck. "What kind of job? Do you have a dog?"

"It's—"

"O.K., children," said Mrs. Bernthal, their teacher. "It's time to clean up."

"Later," said Susanne Lee, hurrying back to her seat.

That evening, as Robert struggled with his math homework, the doorbell rang. Robert heard his mom's voice. "Susanne Lee! How nice to see you!"

What was Susanne Lee doing here? Robert wondered. He came out of his room and thumped down the stairs. Susanne Lee held a small plastic tank in her hands.

"Hi, Robert," she said. "I didn't finish telling you today, but this is the job I have for you."

The tank had a lid with small holes in it. Robert hoped it was on tight. Inside the tank was the biggest, blackest, hairiest spider he had ever seen. It began to move.

Fuzzy

"What is it?" asked Robert. He tried to stay cool.

"It's a tarantula," said Susanne Lee. "Her name is Fuzzy."

"Fuzzy?"

"Yes, she has eight adorable fuzzy legs. See?"

Robert didn't think "adorable" was the right word. Tarantula legs were definitely not adorable.

"Are you going away?" he asked.

"No," said Susanne Lee. "My cat, Fluffy,

is jealous. I'm afraid he'll hurt Fuzzy if I keep her."

How could a monster spider and a killer cat have names like "Fuzzy" and "Fluffy"? "For how long?" asked Robert.

"Um . . . forever?" said Susanne Lee.

Robert opened his mouth, but nothing came out.

"Please?" She smiled sweetly. "Don't be afraid, Robert. She won't hurt you if you are gentle."

Robert swallowed. "I . . . I have to ask my father."

Robert left Susanne Lee standing in the doorway while he went to ask his father if he could keep a tarantula in the house. Of course he would say no. Then that would be that.

Pets were messy. Robert's dad hated any kind of mess. He was so neat and fussy that he turned all the cans in the cupboard face out so he could read the labels.

"Sure," said Mr. Dorfman when Robert explained about Fuzzy.

"Huh?" Robert couldn't believe it.

"You've always wanted a pet," said his dad. "This is a good way for you to have one. It's small enough to keep in your room, and I'm sure you will keep its tank clean."

"Great!" said Susanne Lee when Robert told her. "Here's ten dollars from my birthday money. It's all I have." Then she handed him the tank.

Robert stared at Fuzzy. Her beady eyes stared back at him. She moved her big hairy legs, and Robert felt his skin prickle.

"Feed her once a day. Here's some food." Susanne Lee held out a box, and Robert took it. He didn't ask what was in it. It was bad enough knowing that he had to sleep in the same room as a tarantula.

The Attack of the Giant Tarantula

That night Robert could not sleep. Noises came from the tank on his bookcase. He was sure Fuzzy was trying to get out. He lay there, stiff as a mummy, waiting for the scratching to stop.

Robert was so tired in school the next day that he jumped when Mrs. Bernthal called on him. He missed two easy spelling words on a test and lost his place when they were reading aloud.

"Wake up, Robert. We're on page four," said Mrs. Bernthal.

The next night was even worse. Robert wrapped the covers around him so tightly, he couldn't move his arms and legs.

Scratch, scratch. Robert tried to ignore the sound. He imagined Fuzzy growing into a huge monster—a giant tarantula. She burst out of her tank and jumped onto his bed. *Chomp, chomp.* She chewed through the blankets. Soon she would nibble his toes. Robert tried to swat Fuzzy, but something held his arms down.

He leaped out of bed, tangled in the covers. *Crash!* He knocked over Fuzzy's tank.

Charlie ran in and flipped on the light. "Hey, little bro, what's up?"

"A giant tarantula is loose!" Robert screamed. He leaped back onto his bed, leaving his covers behind.

"Giant tarantula?" said Charlie. "You mean your itty-bitty spider?" Charlie checked under the bed. He looked in Robert's closet.

"There's nothing here," he reported. "Did you check your bed?"

Robert flew off the bed. His bare feet hit the cold floor. He prayed he would not step on anything that moved.

Robert's mom and dad came into his room. "What's going on?" asked Mr. Dorfman.

Robert was so scared, he couldn't talk.

All of a sudden, Charlie burst out laughing.

"What's so funny?" asked Robert.

Charlie pointed to the corner of the room. "I found your giant tarantula."

There was Fuzzy, fast asleep in Robert's slipper.

Buster

After that, Robert was no longer afraid of Fuzzy. He even grew to like her. It was nice having company in his room when he did his homework or played computer games. Now Fuzzy's nighttime noises sounded friendly.

"Tarantulas make good pets," he told Paul at lunch one day. He had just finished reading a book about spiders.

"Don't they bite?" asked Paul.

"Only if you scare them. And you won't die or anything." Robert pulled a piece of bologna out of his sandwich and ate it.

"Hi, Paul." Lester Willis put his tray down and sat next to Robert. "Yo, Robert. I found a big white rabbit in my backyard. Could you keep it?"

"I—I don't know, Lester." Keeping a rabbit was not in Robert's dog-walking plans.

"He's no trouble. I even made him a cage. And I'll pay you."

"How come you can't keep him?"

"My mom says five kids is enough. I'm trying to change her mind."

"I have to ask my mom."

"Cool."

For sure, the answer would be no this time, Robert thought. Rabbits were bigger and probably made bigger messes than tarantulas.

After school, Robert found his mom in the living room. "Mom, Lester wants me to take care of his rabbit."

"That's nice, Rob." Mrs. Dorfman straightened the magazines on the coffee table.

"He wants me to keep it here until he can take it to his house."

His mother stopped fussing with the magazines. "Robert, I know how hard it is to start a new business," she said after a moment. "If the rabbit stays in your room, I think I can convince your father it's O.K."

"Really?"

"Really."

Robert called Lester. "My mom says it's O.K."

Lester let out a hoot. Robert held the phone away from his ear. "I'll be over tonight. My dad can bring me in the truck."

Everyone in Robert's family liked the big white rabbit. "His name is Buster," Lester said.

"He looks like a giant Easter bunny," Robert's dad said.

Mrs. Dorfman held Buster and talked baby talk to him.

"Poor guy must have been in a fight," said Charlie. He pointed to Buster's left ear. It looked like it had been torn.

Lester handed Robert a box of rabbit food. "He also likes carrots."

"O.K.," said Robert, patting Buster's head. Lester's rabbit was the closest thing Robert had ever had to a dog.

Robert's Zoo

One day when Robert got home from feeding the birds, his mom met him at the door. She looked sad. He knew something was wrong.

"Mrs. Glass's daughter called," his mom said. "Mrs. Glass is not getting better. She is going into a nursing home, and they don't allow pets."

"What will happen to Flo and Billie?" Robert asked.

"Mrs. Glass would like you to keep them."

"Really?"

"Yes," said his mom. "Your father can help you get them from her house tomorrow afternoon."

What was wrong with his parents? Suddenly his room was a zoo, and they didn't seem to mind!

The next day, after getting Flo and Billie settled in his room, Robert sank into the sofa in the living room. On TV a news reporter was interviewing a man dressed up as the Easter bunny.

Robert's dad came in and sat down next to him. "Well, Tiger, business is booming, isn't it?"

"I guess," said Robert.

"I think you are showing excellent enterprise."

Robert knew that his dad was giving him a compliment, even though he didn't

know what "enterprise" meant. How could he explain that all he wanted was a dog to play with and instead he'd ended up with a tarantula, two doves, and a rabbit?

"Where does the Easter bunny go to fill his baskets?" said a voice from the TV. It was a commercial for Banbury's Chocolates. Robert turned to look and saw a big white rabbit sitting next to a basket with a yellow bow on the handle. The basket was filled with chocolate bunnies and pink candy eggs. "To Banbury's, of course," the voice continued.

Robert studied the rabbit closely. It looked just like Buster. It even had the same torn ear.

Buster's Surprise

The school bus was coming in five minutes. Robert checked on the animals, as usual. "Good morning, Fuzzy," he said, tapping lightly on her tank. "Good morning, Buster." He looked in Buster's cage and gasped.

"Mom!" he cried. "Come quick!"

Mrs. Dorfman came running. "Oh my," she said. "Oh my, oh my, oh my. Buster had babies."

"But Buster is a boy!"

"Apparently not," said Mrs. Dorfman.

"Don't miss the bus, Rob. We'll deal with this later."

Lester was happy at first to hear the news when Robert told him at lunch. "Seven babies! Way to go, Buster!"

Then Robert reminded him, "Now there are eight rabbits to worry about instead of one."

Lester stopped smiling. "What do I do now?"

Robert wished he knew. "We'll think of something."

"We?" Lester asked.

"Sure." Robert shrugged. "After all, the bunnies were born in my house."

Robert's mom was very clear about what to do. "You have to get rid of them."

"How?"

"Take them to the animal shelter."

"What will they do with them?" Robert asked.

"They'll try to have them adopted."

Robert was afraid to ask the next question. "What happens if they're not adopted?"

"They can't afford to keep all the animals they get," Mrs. Dorfman said. Her voice got softer. "If nobody wants them, they may put them to sleep."

Robert felt like someone had just punched him in the stomach. "You mean forever, right?"

His mom nodded. "The only other way is to find homes for them yourself. If you promise me you'll try to do that, you can keep them until they are big enough to be separated from their mother."

"I promise!" Robert cried. He was sure it would be easy. Everyone would want a bunny.

Emergency Meeting

Robert's mom came into his room with clean laundry to put in his drawers. Bunnies hopped everywhere. One sat on a sock Robert had left on the floor. Another cuddled up against one of his dirty sneakers.

"Rob, you've had these bunnies for a month. They're big enough to leave their mother. Have you found homes for them?"

He and Lester had tried to give them away at school. "Mr. Lobel, the science teacher, is taking one for his classroom."

"That still leaves six," his mom pointed

out. "Plus Buster." Lester's mom would not give in, so Buster needed a home, too.

Robert called the Van Saun Park Zoo. "We have all the rabbits we need," they told him.

Next he called Banbury's Chocolates. What if that white rabbit in their commercial was Buster? Robert got a recording and left a message. Nobody called back.

"I'll drive you over to the animal shelter this weekend," said Mrs. Dorfman. "The longer you put it off, the harder it will be."

Robert called Lester. "We need an emergency meeting," he said. "Tomorrow. Lunchtime."

The next morning was spent on special projects. Mrs. Bernthal had everyone making dioramas for Earth Day. She was going to put them on display in the school lobby.

Paul was busy cutting out strips of aluminum foil. "It's for a river, to run through my rain forest," he told Robert.

Paul could get lost doing anything with art. Robert wished he had something to keep his mind off Buster and her babies.

"Can you come to a meeting at lunchtime?" Robert asked. Paul had good ideas. He and Lester could use his help.

"Sure. What's up?"

"We have to take the rabbits to the animal shelter this weekend," Robert said. "Unless we find homes for them."

At lunchtime Lester was so upset he couldn't eat. "We can let them loose in the park," he said. "And what about the pet store? They sell chicks and ducks and rabbits for Easter."

"In the park they'll be killed or die in no time," said Paul. "And pet stores are even worse. I heard that those animals are treated badly. Kids play with them for a while, then abandon them."

"At least the animal shelter doesn't
starve or hurt them," said Robert. It made
his stomach hurt to say it, but he did.

Lester's shoulders sagged. "Do we have to?" he asked.

"I promised," said Robert.

Lester's mouth trembled. "O.K.," he said.

The Worst Feeling in the World

On Saturday morning, Lester was outside his house waiting when Robert and his mother drove up. He slid into the backseat next to the rabbit cage. Robert was on the other side. Neither of them said a word.

Robert saw Lester take a carrot from his jacket and feed it to Buster. Lester really loved those rabbits.

Robert's mom drove to the animal shelter and parked. "I'll come in with you," she said.

They got out of the car. Lester carried the cage. Robert walked next to him.

Inside, they went up to a woman at the front desk. "We have some rabbits," Lester said.

"To adopt," added Robert.

The woman smiled. "Of course," she said. She picked up a phone and punched some buttons. "We need an attendant," she said.

Soon a young woman in a white coat came out. "Hi," she said. She looked in the cage. "Oh, how sweet."

With one final good-bye, they left the rabbits with the attendant. Lester ran out to the car.

Robert couldn't remember ever feeling worse than he did at that moment.

On the way home, Robert heard a sniffle. Then he realized it was coming from him.

The weekend was long with the rabbits gone from Robert's room. Flo and Billie seemed sad, and Fuzzy hardly moved. Lester called once, just to talk. He choked up when he mentioned Buster's name.

Robert kept busy working on his diorama of a recycling center. He glued a toy car tire onto a pile of others. He made tiny bundles of newspapers, cut from real newspapers, and tied them with thread. He tried not to think about Buster and the baby bunnies at the animal shelter. But the more he tried not to think of them, the more he did.

Charlie saw him working on his diorama. He came into Robert's room to look at it. "Cool," he said. Robert had just glued three soda cans in place. He had painted them blue and marked them ALUMINUM, GLASS, and PLASTIC, just like the ones at the River Edge Recycling Center.

"You forgot the rats," said Charlie.

"Huh?"

"You need rats in it," Charlie told him. "To be more realistic."

"I don't think so," Robert mumbled. He knew better than to listen to his brother. Once Charlie had talked Robert into doing an oral report about the toilet, and everyone had laughed at him.

By Sunday night, Robert's diorama was almost done. He went to bed early. He was tired from not thinking about rabbits.

The Visitor

On Monday, Robert brought his diorama to school. It was almost done, but he still had to paint in the background.

Susanne Lee Rodgers bounced up to Mrs. Bernthal's desk. "My diorama is finished," she said.

"Thank you, Susanne Lee," said Mrs. Bernthal. "You may put your diorama on the window sill." It was the first one completed. Susanne Lee was always the first and the best and the smartest in everything.

The rest of the morning passed slowly. In the afternoon, while they were working on math problems, there was a knock on the door. Mrs. Bernthal opened the door, and a man came in. He carried a red cage with the name BONNIE painted on the side. In his other hand, he carried a shopping bag. He gave Mrs. Bernthal a note.

"Children, this is Mr. Dennis," Mrs. Bernthal announced. "Mr. Dennis trains animals. Say hello to Mr. Dennis, class."

"HELLO, MR. DENNIS," said the children.

"Hello," he said. "I brought my sidekick, Bonnie, with me."

Robert's eyes opened wide as Mr. Dennis took a rabbit out of the cage. It was big and white and had a torn ear, just like Buster.

"Some of you may recognize Bonnie," said Mr. Dennis. "She's on TV."

"I know, I know!" said Melissa Thurm. "She's the Easter bunny!"

"Yes, she's the Easter bunny in the commercial for Banbury's Chocolates."

Robert gasped. "It's Buster!" he said.

"I have a story to tell you about
Bonnie," Mr. Dennis went on. "We filmed a
commercial not far from here. Bonnie got
out of her cage and disappeared. I called

everyone I could think of, but Bonnie was gone and we had to leave."

"That's so sad," said Vanessa Nicolini.

"Yes," said Mr. Dennis. "I thought I would never see Bonnie again. Then, this morning, I got a call from someone at Banbury's Chocolates. They said someone was trying to reach me. He had a rabbit and wondered if it could be Bonnie."

Robert turned to Lester, but Lester had already gone up to the front of the room. He looked the rabbit in the eyes and cried, "Buster!"

"Are you Lester or Robert?" asked Mr. Dennis.

"I'm Lester," said Lester. "Hey! How did you know my name?"

Mr. Dennis laughed. Robert got up, too. "I'm Robert," he said, looking in the cage. Snuggled together were six little bunnies.

The other children came up to pet Bonnie and look at the babies.

"How did you find us?" asked Robert.

"Your mother told me that Lester found Bonnie and that the two of you took care of her. She also told me where I could find Bonnie and your school so that I could come and say thank you."

"You're keeping the babies, too?" Robert asked.

"Yes, unless you'd like to have one," said Mr. Dennis.

"No! Um, thank you," said Robert. "I was just wondering."

"I have treats for everyone," said Mr. Dennis, handing Robert the shopping bag. "Why don't you and Lester hand them out?"

Robert and Lester gave a Banbury's chocolate rabbit to each of their classmates. Mrs. Bernthal got one, too.

"What do you say, class?" asked Mrs. Bernthal.

"THANK YOU, MR. DENNIS!" the class said.

"Mr. Dennis, will you tell us how you train animals?" asked Susanne Lee.

"I'd be glad to," Mr. Dennis answered. He turned to Mrs. Bernthal. "They're smart, aren't they?" he said.

"They're the best class in the whole world," Mrs. Bernthal said.

As Mr. Dennis talked, Robert nibbled at the ears of his chocolate rabbit. He noticed Paul had started at the rabbit's feet. He turned around. Lester had the whole head of his rabbit stuffed in his mouth. Things were definitely back to normal.

As Mr. Dennis talked, Robert let his thoughts wander. Someday he and Paul could become animal trainers like Mr. Dennis. They could start with Fuzzy or with Flo and Billie. He wondered if anyone had ever trained a tarantula to fetch.

Climbing Mountains

A few days later, Mrs. Bernthal had exciting news. "We're going on a class trip," she said, clasping her hands in front of her.

"To the zoo?" asked Melissa. "I'll have to have my allergy shots."

"The science museum!" shouted Brian Hoberman.

"No, no, let's go to see the dinosaurs!" shouted Lester.

"Settle down, children," said Mrs. Bernthal.

Robert secretly hoped it would be the dinosaurs, too. He closed his eyes and

53

tried to send his thoughts to Mrs. Bernthal by mental telepathy. *Dinosaurs. Please, please let it be dinosaurs.* The natural history museum had a new exhibit he was dying to see. His best friend, Paul, was probably wishing just as hard for the planetarium. Paul loved anything to do with space.

"We are going to be one of the first classes to use the new climbing wall in Forest Park," said Mrs. Bernthal.

Robert frowned and opened his eyes.

"What's a climbing wall?" called out Lester.

"It's like the side of a very steep mountain. It has finger- and toeholds, and you have to make your way up the wall," said Susanne Lee Rodgers.

"What if you fall?" asked Melissa. She was afraid of everything.

"You won't fall," said Mrs. Bernthal. "You'll wear a harness that will keep you from falling."

"When are we going?" asked Kevin Kransky.

"A week from next Wednesday," said Mrs. Bernthal. "Have your parents sign this permission form and bring it in by Friday—a week from today." She went around the room handing out slips of paper.

"The climbing wall sounds like fun," said Robert as he and Paul walked home together. They almost always walked, unless it rained. Then they rode the school bus.

"I saw a National Geographic special on mountain climbing," said Paul. "A man got killed. He fell a gazillion feet down the mountain."

"You think the wall's dangerous?" asked Robert.

"They wouldn't let us go if it was. Would they? Let's look at the permission slip."

Robert pulled his permission slip out of his notebook. He read it out loud.

"I give permission for my son/daughter
_____ *to go on a class trip to Forest Park."*

"Farther down," said Paul. "Look." He pointed to the lines at the bottom.

"I will not hold the school responsible for any injury or death that may result from an accident during the trip."

"Injury! Death! It *is* dangerous!"

Paul scratched his head. "But Mrs. Bernthal wouldn't let us do anything that could hurt us."

"Then why do our parents have to sign this?" asked Robert.

"It's probably something the school has to do," said Paul.

"Maybe." Robert wished he could get the picture of the man falling down the mountain out of his head.

Up a Tree

Robert was cat-sitting for Ms. Laney over the weekend. He stopped at her house on his way home. He opened the front door with the key she had given him. Ginger came right up to him with a big *meow*.

Ms. Laney had left three cans of food on the kitchen counter. Robert opened one of the cans and dumped the contents into Ginger's dish. Ginger went right to it when Robert put it down. Then he filled her water dish with fresh water.

While Ginger ate, Robert went out the back door to the yard. He saw a big yellow dog on the other side of the fence. A doghouse stood in the corner of the yard.

"Hi," he said, walking over to the fence.

The dog was on a chain. Its tail wagged furiously. It came over and nuzzled Robert's fingers through the fence with its big pink nose.

Robert looked at the dog's tags. There was one tag to show it had its rabies shot. Another one had a telephone number but no name.

The dog was skinny. Robert searched in his pockets for some kind of food, but all he came up with was a red gummy bear covered with fuzz.

"I have to go now," he said, scratching behind the dog's ears. Robert went back to the house to lock up. But as he opened the back door, Ginger zoomed out.

"Hey!" cried Robert. He ran after her, but the cat climbed up the big apple tree in the yard. She looked down at him from a branch that was way out of reach.

A ladder rested against the tree. Was it for picking apples in the fall, or did Ginger always climb trees? Robert wondered. He started to climb the ladder. On the fourth rung, his legs felt shaky. He let himself down, one rung at a time. When his feet were on the ground again, he felt better.

"Here, Ginger, here, kitty kitty," Robert called. The cat did not move. What should he do? He knew he couldn't leave her there.

Robert went into the house and called his mother. "Stay there," she said. "I'll be right over." Robert sat on the step. Over in the next yard, the yellow dog stared at him through the fence.

Robert's mom had no trouble climbing the ladder. She picked up the cat and climbed back down.

Once Ginger was safely in the house again, Robert walked home with his mom. He told her what had happened on the ladder. "It looked so easy," he said, "until I got up to the fourth rung."

"It's nothing to worry about, Rob," his mom said. "Ladders can feel pretty shaky if you've never been on one."

But if a ladder felt shaky, how would a climbing wall feel?

Fake Ice Cream

Mrs. Bernthal asked everyone in room 204 to bring something to share with the class that had to do with rock climbing.

Charlie had told Robert to take a hanky, in case he had a nosebleed. Robert knew that Charlie liked to tease him, so he didn't listen. Instead he brought a book with lots of pictures of rocks and minerals.

Paul brought a plastic bag and a marker. "Rock climbers use these for collecting specimens," he said.

"What specimens?" asked Matt Blakey. "It's a climbing wall, not real rocks."

"Yes, Matt, that's true," said Mrs. Bernthal. "But there's nothing wrong with pretending. Thank you, Paul."

Susanne Lee brought survival food. "Astronauts eat this kind of food, too," she explained. "It doesn't weigh much or take up much room, so it's good for long trips to places where you might not find food."

She opened a silver-colored pouch. "This is strawberry ice cream," she said, showing the class. Inside the pouch were dry brown cubes. They didn't look anything like strawberry ice cream.

Susanne Lee broke up the cubes into tiny pieces so everyone could have a taste. Robert made a face as he touched his sample with the tip of his tongue. Hmmm. It tasted good. He licked it again. It really did taste like strawberry ice cream!

He put the rest of the sample in his mouth and ate it. Maybe a pocketful of those cubes would be fun to take along on a rock-climbing trip. Susanne Lee knew everything.

The trip to the climbing wall was still a week away. Robert wanted to go, but he kept thinking of his shaky knees on that ladder. Should he tell Mrs. Bernthal? What if she made him stay home?

When he got home from school, Robert's mom was on the phone. She sounded pretty upset. "Don't go near it if it comes back," she said into the telephone.

Robert happened to look out the window at their yard. A big yellow dog was sniffing the grass. "Mom!" he called.

"It could be sick or carrying a disease," his mom said into the phone.

"Mom!" Robert said again.

"Just a minute, Robert," said Mrs. Dorfman while she held her hand over the receiver. "I'm talking on the phone."

"I know, but . . ." Robert's mom signaled to him to be quiet. She continued her conversation. Robert went out to the yard. The dog came right up to him and licked his hand. Robert scratched behind the dog's ears.

"Robert!" cried his mom moments later, opening the door to the yard. "Be careful! That must be the stray dog Mrs. Rudner called me about. He could be dangerous!"

"That's what I was trying to tell you," said Robert, bending down and holding out his hand. "I know this dog. It's the one that was chained up next-door to Ms. Laney's."

A Matter of Life or Death

Robert looked at the dog's collar. The tags were gone, including the one with the phone number. Maybe the dog's chain had broken, and the tags had fallen off. "I wonder how he got loose," Robert said.

"I'll call the sheriff," Robert's mom said as she went inside. "He'll know what to do."

The dog was still in the yard, lying at Robert's feet, when the sheriff arrived. He wagged his tail as the sheriff approached.

"Several people in the area have called

about this dog," said the sheriff to Mrs. Dorfman. "He belongs to Sam Pratt. Sam says he doesn't want him back. Said we might as well shoot him."

"*Shoot* him?" cried Robert, holding on to the dog. "You can't do that!"

"It would be a shame," said the sheriff. "He seems like a nice enough dog. Let's see if the animal shelter can take him."

The shelter! Robert would never forget the close call he had had with the bunnies at the shelter.

The sheriff went over to his car and called something in on the radio.

"Mom, can he really shoot the dog?" Robert asked.

"I don't know, Rob."

The sheriff came back. "Well," he said, "the shelter is full. They'll clean him up and give him his shots so they can place

him in a foster home, but they have to find one right away. They can keep him overnight, but that's all."

"What's a foster home?" asked Robert.

"A family that will take care of the dog until they find him a permanent home."

Robert looked at his mom hopefully.

"No," she said. "No dogs, Robert."

Robert sighed. It was the same old story. He could take care of other people's pets, and even have pets of his own if they were neat and tidy and could be kept in his room. But that did not include dogs.

The sheriff took the dog by the collar and led him away.

The Deal

Robert could usually eat two burritos. That night he could barely finish one. He even skipped the chocolate pudding with whipped cream on top for dessert. He fed Fuzzy, his tarantula, and Flo and Billie, the doves. Then he did his homework and went to bed early.

His parents came in together to say good night. It had been a long time since both his mom *and* dad had tucked him in.

"Rob?"

"Mmmm?"

"Rob, your father and I want to talk to you."

"O.K." He sat up.

"It's about that dog."

Robert sat up straighter. "What about him?"

"We've been talking," said his mom. "Your father and I agree that you have been an excellent pet-sitter."

"Excellent," his father repeated.

Robert's heart beat faster.

"And you kept your promise about the bunnies," said his mother.

"We feel you deserve something special for your hard work," said Mr. Dorfman.

What were they trying to say? Robert thought he would pop if they didn't hurry up and tell him.

"If you want to take in that dog until he is adopted, it's O.K. with us," said his mom.

Robert rubbed his eyes. Was he asleep and dreaming? He couldn't believe it.

"We will all try really hard to get along with this idea." Mrs. Dorfman looked at her husband. Mr. Dorfman looked uncertain, but he didn't object.

"And you'll have to do your part," Robert's dad added.

"What's my part?"

"You'll have to train the dog so he is adoptable."

"O.K."

"This is temporary. You will have to give him up when the time comes. You understand that, don't you?"

Robert remembered the dog's cold nose on his fingers. He remembered the dog's brown eyes that sparkled when he petted him. Most dogs didn't grin, but this one did, whenever he saw Robert.

"Yes, yes!" he said. He finally had a dog. A real, live dog!

The next day after Robert got out of school, all three of them went to the animal shelter to get the dog. A man in a white lab coat brought the dog out. The dog's tail wagged when he spotted Robert.

"I'm Dr. Hudson," said the vet. "You've got a healthy dog here. He's been cleaned up, and he's got all his shots."

As they started to leave the vet's office, the dog lifted his leg on Dr. Hudson. Robert gasped.

"I guess he's not housebroken," said Dr. Hudson. "You're going to have to work on this guy. He's old for adoption—he's about two. You've got to make him adoptable."

"What does that mean, exactly?" asked Robert.

"It means he must go to the bathroom *outdoors*." Dr. Hudson looked down at his pants. "It means he can't chew and destroy

things that are not his. He must understand simple commands like 'sit' and
'stay.' He should also recognize his name
and come when he's called." The vet bent

down to pat the dog. "What did you say his name was?"

"I didn't," said Robert. "We don't have a name for him yet."

"Well," Dr. Hudson said, "as I remember, Sam just called him 'Dog.' When you give him a real name and he starts to understand it, it will be easier to train him."

"O.K."

"Don't forget the housebreaking," said Dr. Hudson.

Second Thoughts?

Mr. Dorfman had hardly opened the door before the dog pulled Robert past him and inside.

"Hey! I'm supposed to be pulling you!" said Robert.

The dog sniffed the corner of Mr. Dorfman's leather recliner and lifted his leg.

"No!" cried Robert and Mr. Dorfman at the same time. But it was too late.

Robert saw a little vein in his dad's neck pop out. His mom's hands went to her cheeks as the dog's tail swept over the coffee table, barely missing a crystal polar bear.

"I'll take him out," said Robert before anyone told him to. He and the dog dashed out the back door and into the yard.

Robert let the dog off the leash. The dog went right to a bush at the far end of the yard and sniffed all around it.

This was not going to be easy, Robert thought. He had to work fast, or his parents might have second thoughts about being a foster family.

That evening Robert took the dog out to the yard every hour, with broken dog biscuits jammed in his pocket. He read once that dogs should be rewarded with treats or pats every time they did something right.

By ten o'clock, Robert was so tired he could hardly move his feet up the stairs to

his room. He got into his pajamas and was just about to spread newspapers over the floor, when the dog lifted his leg on Robert's beanbag chair, the one he and Paul always sat in.

"NO!" Robert screamed. He grabbed the dog by the collar and, barefoot, dragged him downstairs and into the yard. The dog was so startled, his ears were flattened against his head. He whimpered.

"I'm sorry, boy," Robert said, scratching the dog behind the ears. The grass was cold and wet on Robert's bare feet. "It's not your fault. But we are going to be in big trouble if you don't get housebroken soon."

The dog nuzzled Robert's hand. They went back inside. Robert wished on a star that night. He crossed his fingers, too.

The Great Pepperoni

The next morning Robert dragged himself out of bed. He put his foot over the side, and it landed on something soft and furry.

It wasn't a dream! There really was a dog in his room. The dog was looking up at Robert and wagging his tail. Robert held his breath as he looked for signs of puddles. There were none! The newspapers were dry.

"Does he have a name?" asked Charlie, coming into his room. He threw a rubber ball to the dog. The dog jumped as the ball hit him on the nose.

"Not yet," said Robert.

"Well," said Charlie, "this dog can really handle a ball."

"He . . . he'll learn." Robert wished he could go back to bed.

"Yeah, and you'll pitch for the Yankees next year!" Charlie teased. Robert wasn't very good at most sports.

Then Charlie bounced the ball off Robert's head.

"Hey!" yelled Robert.

The dog stood up and barked at Charlie. Charlie jumped back. "O.K., O.K.!" he said, leaving Robert's room.

Robert turned around just in time to see the dog lifting his leg on the wall.

"Oh no!" he cried. If only he had taken him outside right away. Robert dressed in a hurry and brought the dog down to the yard. He filled a bowl with water and put it on the ground. He went off to school with sleep still in his eyes.

That morning Mrs. Bernthal talked more about the wall-climbing trip. Robert tried to pay attention, but he kept daydreaming about what he would name the dog. He wrote one name after another in his notebook and showed it to Paul. *Rex. Rocky. Homer. Bones.* None of them seemed right.

Coming home was just as he dreamed it would be. The second he walked into the yard, the dog ran up to him and slobbered him with kisses. His tail worked back and forth like the windshield wipers on Mr. Dorfman's car.

Homework could wait. It was Friday. Robert stayed in the yard, and he and the dog played tug of war with a stick. Then Robert practiced the "sit," "lie down," and "stay" commands. Each time the dog got it right, Robert gave him a small piece of dog biscuit.

"Stay" was the hardest. Every time Robert walked away, the dog got up to follow him.

After a while they went in. Robert's mom and dad were looking at the paper. Charlie was messing with the VCR.

"Where is that pizza?" said Mr. Dorfman, checking his watch.

Robert's mom read the box from the videotape Charlie chose. "*The Attack of the Aliens*. Don't you guys ever choose anything that isn't silly or disgusting?"

The doorbell rang. The dog jumped up and barked.

"Well, he's a good watchdog, anyway," said Robert's mom as she answered the door. She paid the deliveryman and brought in the box of pizza.

The dog nearly went berserk. He ran in circles. He whined. He panted. He looked like he would explode at any second.

"Mom, he's hungry," said Charlie.

"He can't be," said Robert's mom. "He ate a whole bowl of dog food earlier." She put the pizza box down on the dining room table.

The dog stared up at the pizza box, drooling.

"He sure knows about pizza," said Robert, sitting down at the table. He opened the box, tore a tiny piece off the pizza, and tossed it to the dog. The dog swallowed it whole.

"Sit!" said Robert. The dog sat. Robert tossed him a piece of pepperoni off the pizza. "Good boy!" he said, scratching the dog behind his ears.

"It's not good to feed the dog from the table," said Mr. Dorfman. He cut up his slice with a knife and fork.

Robert was pretty hungry himself. He bit into his slice. The dog drooled, watching him.

"I've got it! Pepperoni!" he shouted.

"Yes, it is," said his mom. "Isn't that what you always ask for?"

"Not the pizza! The dog! Pepperoni! That's his name!"

"The Great Pepperoni! It sounds like a magic act," said Charlie.

Pepperoni's tail thumped on the floor. Robert tossed him another bite of his slice. His dad frowned.

"Oops. I'm sorry," said Robert.

"Well," said Robert's mom, "I hope one of the first things you do is make his mistakes disappear."

"I'll train him with pizza!" said Robert.

"What happens when you run out of pizza?" asked Charlie.

"I guess I'll have to get more."

Pepperoni barked. He seemed to think that was a fine idea.

Deep, Deep Trouble

On Saturday the newspapers on the floor in Robert's room were dry again. Robert didn't wait to get dressed. He put on his slippers. "Come on, Pepperoni," he called.

He ran downstairs with Pepperoni at his heels and grabbed a plastic bag filled with leftover pizza cut up into small bites. The minute they were in the yard, Pepperoni lifted his leg against the fence.

"Good dog!" yelled Robert. He ran over to Pepperoni and gave him a piece of pizza. He scratched his ears. He kissed his face. "Oh, please," Robert begged. "Please be housebroken!" Pepperoni wagged his tail as if he understood.

Later that day Robert was in his room on his beanbag chair reading a book about mountain climbing. Pepperoni lay across his feet. The book had pictures of people on ropes hanging by their fingertips over great canyons. He imagined himself dangling on the ropes as rocks tumbled down all around him.

"Robert!"

His father's voice broke his concentration. He put the book down and went to the window overlooking the yard.

"What, Dad?"

"I think you'd better get down here," he answered. "This yard is becoming a minefield of dog pretzels."

Robert thumped down the stairs in his sneakers and went out to the yard. His dad was wiping something off his shoe.

"Oh," he said, understanding what the problem was. He went inside to look for plastic bags.

The bags came in all sizes. Robert was sure the snack size would be too small. The gallon size was too big. He took one quart size and one sandwich size.

Robert picked up all the dog pretzels he could find. He wished he had a third hand to hold his nose while he used his other hands to scoop and bag. Now he knew that having a dog had its downside.

On Monday, Robert dressed in a hurry. Pepperoni watched him. "Hold on, boy." They made it to the yard without an accident. Robert hugged Pepperoni extra hard before he left for school.

Robert was glad his mom had made arrangements with her partner at the travel agency to do some of her work from home. While she worked in her little office upstairs, Pepperoni had company. And when Robert got home from school, it was nice to know his mom was there.

At twenty past three, the school bus stopped on Robert's corner. He got off. He'd taken the bus so he could get home to Pepperoni faster. He unlatched the back-yard gate, but Pepperoni wasn't there. He went into the house.

"Mom? Where's Pepperoni?"

Mrs. Dorfman came out of her upstairs office and stood at the top of the stairs. She took off her glasses.

"Pepperoni is in the upstairs bathroom," she told him. "He's being punished."

"Why? What did he do?" Robert asked.

"He dug up my flower bed. There are deep trenches where my petunias used to be." She didn't yell. She spoke calmly, but her hair was coming undone.

The bathroom looked like a snowstorm had hit it. Toilet paper was everywhere. Some of it was shredded. Some was draped on Pepperoni. Pepperoni's mouth was bright red.

"Pepperoni! What did you do?" Robert saw his mom's makeup bag on the floor, with the lipstick container open and empty. Pepperoni must have eaten the lipstick part. As Robert straightened the fluffy blue bath mat, he saw that it had been chewed up.

"Oh no." Robert sank down onto the floor. He tried to clean the lipstick off Pepperoni's mouth, but Pepperoni still looked like a circus clown. He climbed on Robert and covered him with wet kisses.

After he cleaned up the mess, Robert took Pepperoni downstairs into the yard.

"How can I make you understand?" he said as the dog nuzzled his hand. "We are in deep, deep trouble!"

This card certifies that *Pepperoni* the dog is officially HOUSEBROKEN.

The Photo

"**P**epperoni is housebroken, I think," said Robert as he and Paul ate their lunch the next day.

"That's great," said Paul.

Robert yawned. He had spent yesterday afternoon helping his mom fix the flower beds that were ruined. He picked up dog pretzels with his new pooper-scooper. After dinner and homework, he practiced his commands with Pepperoni.

"So what can he do now?" asked Paul.

"He can sit, and stay, and lie down," said Robert. "I can't get him to roll over, but I'm working on it."

"Does he come when you call him?"

"No," Robert said, disappointed. "He doesn't seem to get that."

"Even when you feed him pizza?"

"Even when I feed him pizza," said Robert.

"Well, I think you did a lot," said Paul. "He's a great dog, and it sounds like he almost always behaves."

"I guess," said Robert. The way Paul said it, it didn't sound so bad. Then he remembered his mom's face when she'd told him about her petunias.

"My parents have been really good," he said. "But I never know what's going to happen next. If Pepperoni does anything like chewing something or digging up the flower bed again, they're going to crack."

Robert had heard that line in a movie. It seemed to fit right now.

Before they went home, Mrs. Bernthal reminded them about the class trip the next day. "Remember to wear shoes with rubber soles that have a good grip," she said. "And bring lunch and snacks. We'll be out most of the day."

When Robert got home, Pepperoni was curled up on his bed. He flopped down next to the dog and buried his head in Pepperoni's fur.

Robert's mom knocked. "Phone call for you, Rob," she said. "It's someone named Annie, over at the animal shelter."

Robert picked up the phone in the upstairs hall. "Hello?"

"How are you doing with your dog?" Annie asked.

"He has a name now. Pepperoni."

"That's a neat name," said Annie. "And how is Pepperoni doing?"

Robert told her everything Pepperoni had learned. He didn't want Annie to think he wasn't doing his job. "I've been training him with pizza."

"Wonderful," said Annie. "Do you think he's adoptable?"

"Oh . . . I . . . don't know," said Robert. The question surprised him. He needed more time.

"Well, here's the thing. We thought we'd put a picture of Pepperoni in the local paper. If we show his picture and say something nice about him, someone may be interested in adopting him."

"O.K.," said Robert. "I'll take his picture."

"Great. Take a few shots, if you can. We'll need them by Friday to get in the next issue. We'll put one in that really shows him off as something special. Don't worry. It sounds like you're doing a great job. Someone is going to get a terrific dog."

Yes. Someone is. Robert just wished he were the someone.

Robert had an almost full roll of film in his camera, and that night he used it up on Pepperoni. He took pictures of Pepperoni sitting, standing, lying down, sleeping, and eating. He took pictures of Pepperoni on his bed, in the yard, and under the coffee table in the living room.

Finally, feeling tired and silly, he started dressing Pepperoni up for the last few pictures. Charlie walked by and joined in. First Pepperoni wore Charlie's Yankees baseball cap, and then he wore Robert's earmuffs. Next they put Mom's sunglasses on him and dressed him in Dad's barbecue apron and chef's hat. They laughed until their sides were sore. Even Pepperoni seemed to be laughing as he rolled over on his back for a belly rub.

Mount Everest, Here I Come!

The class was in high spirits on the bus to Forest Park. The girls, as usual, started to sing. The boys, as usual, pretended they couldn't stand the noise.

"Quack, quack, quaaaaack!" croaked Lester Willis, flapping his arms like wings. The other boys covered their ears and made faces.

Robert and Paul ignored the noise and compared sneakers. They had made sure to follow Mrs. Bernthal's instructions about what shoes to wear. Paul's had a lot of spiky things on the bottom. Robert's had treads like car tires.

At Forest Park, a guide led the class to the climbing wall. He wore a brown ranger's hat and a green uniform. The words *Park Service* were sewn on his sleeve.

"It's thirty feet tall," he told them, "or about three stories high. There are finger- and toeholds built into it. They are small— some of them too small for much of a grip—but the challenge is to find a hold and get enough leverage to help you advance up the wall. You will be wearing a harness that's attached to the wall by a rope when you climb, so you won't get hurt if you slip. Two of you can climb at the same time. Just follow my instructions. You have to trust me."

Robert waited his turn in line. He watched as Paul, in front of him, put the harness on. He felt a little like he would throw up as he moved to the first place in line. That wall looked pretty high, and it was straight up. Mountains were on a slant, weren't they? He could hardly see the finger- and toeholds from where he stood.

Now Matt Blakey was on the wall. He seemed to be in a hurry to get to the top.

"Slow down," the guide called to Matt. "Think about each step carefully."

Paul was halfway up the wall.

"That's right, son, you've got it," the guide called after him.

Robert thought about what the guide had said. You had to trust him to climb the wall. That's how Pepperoni learned, by trusting Robert. They took one step at a time. Robert trusted the guide. He would do just what he said and think about each move he made.

"Oops!" Matt lost his footing. He swung in the harness until he got his footing again. Well, at least you couldn't fall off the wall and get killed.

Paul was down on the ground again. He got out of the harness and gave Robert a thumbs-up. The guide helped Robert into the harness next. "Way to go, Robert!" called Lester. Robert tried to smile, to show he wasn't afraid.

"All right," said the guide. "Find a place on the wall you can grab onto with your right hand."

Robert felt around with his fingers. He stretched way to the right and up. He found a place where his fingers fit into a small space. He held on.

"Now find a place for your left foot," said the guide.

The toe of Robert's sneaker scraped the wall until he found one.

"Now find another hold for your left hand, and then your other foot."

Robert swallowed hard and concentrated. He lifted his foot off the ground. He held on as he searched the wall with his toe. One place was too small. He needed a better place to put his toe. He found it.

"Good. You've got the idea," said the guide. "Keep going, one move at a time."

Robert found one toehold or fingerhold after another and started his way up the wall. At one point, his knees began to tremble. Robert remembered his mom telling him it was natural to be a little shaky on the ladder because he had never used one before. He had never been on a climbing wall before, either. He kept going. Soon his knees stopped shaking.

When he reached the top, Robert felt so good he looked down at his classmates on the ground.

"Don't look," called the guide. Robert knew why he said that. Robert's head swam,

and he had to close his eyes to stop being dizzy. "Climb down just as you climbed up," said the guide. "One step at a time."

Robert eased down, his fingers and toes searching for one place after another. The rope was right there, attached to his harness. He knew it would save him from falling if he slipped. At last one foot landed on the ground. Robert jumped off the wall. His knees felt like jelly, but he had done it.

On the bus ride back to school, the girls were too tired even to sing, and the boys were quiet, too. Robert couldn't wait to tell his parents that he had climbed the wall. And to curl up with Pepperoni.

A Home for Pepperoni

More than a week had gone by. When Robert got home from school, Pepperoni greeted him with his tail wagging. His parents weren't there, but the house didn't seem so empty now.

Robert noticed a note from his mom on the kitchen table.

Rob,

Had to run over to the mall to pick up some papers from the office. Be right back.

Mom

The latest issue of *The Guide,* a free local paper, lay on the kitchen table with the rest of the mail. He opened it to the section where pets were offered for sale or adoption.

"Look!" he shouted, forgetting that no one was around. Pepperoni's picture, in the apron and chef's hat, was at the top of the page. Robert read out loud: *"Yellow Lab mix. Good family dog. Pepperoni loves pizza and is affectionate and gentle."* Robert never expected them to use one of the silly pictures. Wait until Charlie saw it!

Now all they had to do was wait and see if anyone responded.

Upstairs, Robert dropped his book bag from his shoulder. Friday! He had all weekend to ride his bike and play with Pepperoni.

The phone rang. Robert picked up the extension in the hall. It was Annie.

"A man named Pietro Gardini saw Pepperoni's picture," she said. "Can we come over this evening so he can meet Pepperoni?"

Robert's stomach twisted into one big knot. It was too soon. He needed more time with Pepperoni. He still had to teach him to come when he called his name. He still had to buy him that huge rawhide bone he had seen in the pet store. He still had to make Pepperoni a perfect dog so he would find the perfect home.

"My parents aren't here now," he said. "But I guess it's O.K." He wished he could just say, "No! I'm not ready!" but he couldn't.

"O.K., thanks," said Annie. "We'll be over around eight o'clock. Tell your parents when they come home."

"O.K., I will." Robert hung up, dragged himself into his room, and sank into his beanbag chair. Pepperoni lay at his feet, his chin resting on Robert's sneakers. They stayed that way for a long time.

Shortly after the pizza was finished and the video of *Doctor Slime* had been put in the VCR, the doorbell rang. Pepperoni barked, and Mrs. Dorfman got up to open the door.

"Come in, please," she said, showing them in. "It's so nice to meet you, Mr. Gardini."

"Please call me Pete," he said, extending a hand. Mrs. Dorfman shook it and smiled.

"Ah, and this must be Pepperoni!" Pete got down on one knee. Pepperoni gave him a slobbery kiss. "I think we are going to be friends." Robert felt a little jealous.

Mr. Dorfman showed Annie and Pete to the dining room, and they sat down.

"I am opening a new restaurant," Pete said, "on Route 4. Pete's Pizza Palace. I want people to come there with the whole family.

When I saw Pepperoni's picture, with the hat and the apron, and read that he loves pizza, it gave me an idea."

Pete leaned over and smiled. "I will use this dog for my logo."

"What's a logo?" asked Robert, glancing at Annie. She winked at him. Maybe she didn't know what it was, either.

"It's a picture or a symbol. My logo will be a picture of a dog in a chef's hat and an apron. We will put it in all our ads and on our napkins and pizza boxes. People will see it and know that my restaurant is a friendly place where they can bring the whole family."

Robert frowned. "But where will Pepperoni *live?*"

Pete stopped smiling. "Oh no," he said. "I'm sorry. I gave you the wrong impression. I want the dog for my family. We lost our dog, Pavarotti, about a month ago."

Pete's voice got sad. "He was fourteen years old, part of our family. My wife and children cried for days. When I saw the picture of Pepperoni in the paper, I thought he would make a good dog for my family. It was after we decided to adopt him that I got the idea for the logo. I kept looking at the picture. It made me laugh."

Robert felt better. He liked Pete. He knew he and Pepperoni would get along just fine. Pete's family was probably pretty nice, too. But he didn't feel ready to give up his dog.

His dog! Robert had never thought of Pepperoni as his dog before. He loved him, and he loved having him around, but he always knew Pepperoni would someday have a different owner.

"Pete, are you ready to take him now?" asked Annie.

Robert almost stopped breathing.

"Yes, that would be fine. He can come home with me tonight. My family will be so happy."

Robert got up. "Excuse me. I need a drink of water." He went to the kitchen. Pepperoni followed him. He got down on the floor and let the dog slobber him with kisses. He hugged him hard, scratching behind his ears. "I love you, Pepperoni," he whispered into the dog's ear. Pepperoni licked his nose.

"Pepperoni," called Annie. The dog's ears perked up. "Come here, boy." Robert let go, and Pepperoni bounced into the living room. Robert followed him, his mouth open.

"He did it!" he said.

"Did what?" asked Annie.

"He came when you called his name. He's never done that before!"

Annie and Pete looked up from some papers. "Ah, you have done a great job," said Pete. "Annie just told me you trained him to be a good dog."

It was hard to speak. "Can I . . . would it be O.K. . . . ." Robert couldn't get it out.

"Of course. Come to visit Pepperoni anytime," said Pete. "We would like that. Here is our address." He wrote something on a card and handed it to Robert. Then he reached into his jacket pocket. "And always, there will be a big welcome for you when you visit my restaurant." He handed a couple of coupons to Mrs. Dorfman.

"Free pizza!" she exclaimed. "How nice!"

Annie and Pete were ready to leave. Pepperoni looked confused.

"You're going with Pete," said Robert. "I'll see you soon." He gave Pepperoni's ears one last scratch. "And I'll bring you that rawhide bone. You be a good boy, hear?"

Pepperoni slurped a big kiss across Robert's hand.

When they had gone, Robert and his parents went back to the living room, where Charlie was rewinding the movie. "You missed some great scenes," he said.

"Oh, I wouldn't say that," said Robert's mom. Her voice sounded funny. Sure enough, her eyes were filled with tears.

Robert thought of Pepperoni as he had first seen him—just a skinny, neglected dog. Now Pepperoni was ready to live in a home where he would be loved. And he would never be far away from a pizza treat. It was time to let him go, and even his mom was sad.

"How are you doing, Tiger?" asked Robert's dad.

Surprised, Robert looked at his dad. His eyes weren't filled with tears, but he sounded sad, too.

They would all miss Pepperoni. But how could it have worked out any better? And maybe the next time he asked for a dog, his parents wouldn't say no so fast.

"I'm O.K., Dad," he said. "I'm really O.K."

BARBARA SEULING is a well-known author of books for children and is busy writing more stories about her hero, Robert Dorfman. She divides her time between New York City and Vermont.

PAUL BREWER likes to draw gross, silly situations, which is why he enjoys working on books about Robert so much. He lives in San Diego, California, with his wife and two daughters.